To: Peter and Sandy.

Hope you enjoy.

Love.

# Dear Liza

A NOVEL BY

## Sydney Banks

Lone Pine Publishing

This novel is a work of fiction. All names, characters and incidents are the
product of the author's imagination. Any resemblance to actual events or
persons, living or dead, is entirely coincidental.

**The Publisher: Lone Pine Publishing**

10145 – 81 Avenue                          1808 B Street NW, Suite 140
Edmonton, AB, Canada  T6E 1W9              Auburn, WA, USA  98001

**Website:** www.lonepinepublishing.com


**Library and Archives Canada Cataloguing in Publication**

Banks, Sydney
    Dear Liza : a novel / by Sydney Banks.

ISBN-13: 978-1-55105-332-5.--ISBN-10: 1-55105-332-2

    I. Title.

PS8553.A57D42 2004          C813'.54          C2004-906378-2


*Editorial Director:* Nancy Foulds
*Project Editor:* Gary Whyte
*Production Manager:* Gene Longson
*Design & Layout:* Curtis Pillipow
*Cover Design:* Gerry Dotto

We acknowledge the financial support of the Government of Canada
through the Book Publishing Industry Development Programme (BPIDP)
for our publishing activities.

*PC: P1*

# Table of Contents

Chapter One      Meeting Liza .................................. 5

Chapter Two      Laura's Reaction ...................... 13

Chapter Three    Returning to the Bridge ........ 20

Chapter Four     Meeting Jenny ........................... 24

Chapter Five     Cookie ......................................... 38

Chapter Six      Laura's Awakening .................. 49

Chapter Seven   The Millers ................................. 57

Chapter Eight    A New Home ............................. 63

Chapter Nine     Liza Falls Ill ................................. 77

# Chapter 1

# Meeting Liza

October of the year 1834 arrived in London, bringing with it the sort of weather one would normally expect a bit later in the year—damp, mercilessly cold and downright miserable. A heavy fog shrouded the city. The fine mist that filled the air wormed its way down collars, into boots and through coats, wetting those unfortunate enough to be abroad on the streets as surely as a downpour.

As Major David Rutherford stepped out of his carriage, a doorman in the dark livery of a London gentlemen's club approached him with an umbrella. "Good morning, Sir. Mind the steps, they're a might slippery."

The Major slipped quickly through the heavy, oak door of the club premises and removed his wrap. As he made his way toward his favourite armchair, Colonel George Oliver Michael, an old acquaintance he hadn't seen for a considerable time, greeted him. Extending his hand, the Colonel smiled, "Jolly good to see you again, David. You're looking well."

They sat before the fire and talked for some time. Then the Colonel enquired, "How are your parents these days?"

"I'm afraid both my parents died six months ago in a boating accident."

A look of deep concern passed over the Colonel's face. "Oh! I'm so sorry to hear that, old man. What in heaven's name happened?"

"Nobody really knows for sure. Apparently, they were out on the lake when a sudden storm blew in, and we imagine that their boat was swamped."

"Jolly bad luck, old man," said the Colonel, shaking his head. "Damned shame, if you ask me. I had heard you gave up your commission and are now Major David Rutherford, Retired. I presume your leaving His Majesty's service is related to your parents' untimely death?"

"Yes, I had to take over the family business when my father died, and it takes all my time to run the estate. To tell you the truth, I was about ready to say goodbye to the army and spend some time enjoying England.

"Laura is going to be pleased when she learns

we met at the club and that you're here for a while," Major Rutherford continued. "You must come see us one afternoon. Our grandchildren will be delighted to meet Colonel George Oliver Michael of His Majesty's Royal Guards."

The Colonel asked, "And those children of yours, how old are they now?"

"Elizabeth is twenty-six and Roger was thirty years old last June."

"By George, how time flies," said the Colonel. "It seems like just yesterday that Elizabeth was born. Damn good celebration in the mess that night. I shall never forget how we hid the old Colonel's horse and he was so outraged he swore he'd put the culprit or culprits up against the wall and shoot them.

"And what about that good-looking younger sister of yours, David, how is she doing?"

"Alice is still happily married to a barrister here in London," replied the Major. "As a matter of fact, I have an appointment with my brother-in-law and I'm afraid I'm already ten minutes late."

The Major got up to leave. "Why don't you pop 'round some day and have tea with us, Colonel? You know where we live, and I'm certain that Laura will be overjoyed to see you again."

"Delighted! I'll try for next week, old man."

* * *

The appointment with his brother-in-law lasted longer than the Major expected, and listening to what he considered to be legal gibberish left him thoroughly exhausted. At best he was lucky if he could understand fifty percent of what the lawyer said. After what seemed an eternity, the church bells chimed two o'clock. The business meeting concluded and he was looking forward to the hour's ride home. The Major stepped out of the law offices to find his coachman, Robert, waiting with the carriage. They set off without delay, but as they approached London Bridge the horse threw a shoe, sending Robert into a state of anxiety bordering on panic.

"Sorry, Sir, but we'll have to take Nell to a blacksmith and have him fix her shoe."

"Have you any idea how long that will take?" the Major asked.

"No more than an hour, Sir, if the smithy isn't busy. Perhaps I can get you another carriage to take you home."

"Don't worry about it, Robert. Tell me, would you know if there is a tavern nearby where I can get some food and ale?"

"Yes, Sir, there's one just up the way called The Old Cock Pheasant, but Major, Sir, it isn't the kind of place that a gentleman would frequent."

Ignoring Robert's warning, the Major informed him that he wanted to stretch his legs a little and get some fresh air.

Reaching into a box beneath the driver's seat, Robert pulled out a pistol and offered it to the Major, explaining that the neighbourhood was full of undesirable and unscrupulous people.

"I don't think I'll require that. Just pick me up at The Old Cock Pheasant when you are finished."

As the Major made his way through the crowded street and walked toward the River Thames, he was forced to veer first right then left to miss the muddier sections and to avoid collisions with the horse carts and hand barrows hurrying along the busy street. Suddenly, he realized that for the first time in his life he was afoot on the mean streets of London near the Thames. After a short walk, he came upon The Old Cock Pheasant Inn and was delighted to discover an establishment far more pleasant and comfortable than Robert had described. Seating himself at a table, he called to the landlord his order of ale, bread and cheese. An hour passed with no sign of Robert. Assuming there must have been complications at the blacksmith's, the Major asked the innkeeper to inform his coachman that he had taken a stroll and to wait at the tavern until he returned.

The Major set out once again to explore the busy backstreets of the city near the river. He was horrified by the appalling appearance of some of the local inhabitants. Suddenly he felt something tugging at his jacket sleeve. Looking down, he saw a little girl with a magnificent head of shiny blond hair that surrounded and enhanced her bright blue eyes. The rest of her appearance, however, was not nearly so appealing. Her frock, which seemed to have been made for a much larger child, hung down to her ankles. It was clean, but showed years of wear, the colours had faded to a motley brown and her mud-spattered shoes were worn beyond repair.

In a gentle voice she asked the Major, "Sir, would you like to buy my beautiful brass candle-stick? Only a penny ha'penny?"

Before he could answer, someone grabbed the child's arm. It was Robert.

"Away with you, you young guttersnipe, away with you or I'll give you the back of my hand." Robert turned to the Major, "Don't trust her, Sir, she probably stole it; they're all the same in this neighbourhood. I tell you, Sir, you have to be care-ful around these parts."

Pulling herself up to her full height, the girl chal-lenged Robert. "You have no right to say such a thing! I didn't steal the candlestick. I am an honest girl, I am. My mother always told me to be honest, and you have no right to accuse me of stealing. I found it on the mudflats and it took me two whole days to get it so shiny." With these words she pro-ceeded to polish the candlestick on her dress.

Looking at the poor little soul, the Major felt in his heart that the child was telling the truth. Reaching into his pocket he handed her two pennies. The sight of the money made her eyes light up like blue candles.

"Thank you Sir, thank you, but all I have is a farthing, I don't have enough change."

"Just keep the change," the Major replied.

Robert was greatly disturbed by the Major's

purchase, especially his generosity when he gave her the extra halfpenny, and couldn't resist speaking. "If you don't mind me saying so, Sir, that's a lot of money to give to someone like her and I'd bet a king's ransom that the little street urchin has a halfpenny change somewhere."

Ignoring Robert's cynical remarks, the Major asked the girl, "What is your name, child?"

"Liza, Sir. Liza Adams."

"Do your parents live around here?"

"I have no parents, Sir, they are both in heaven."

Her answer surprised the Major, and for a moment he remained speechless, then he asked her, "Who takes care of you?"

"Nobody, Sir, I take care of myself and Jenny."

"And who is Jenny?" the Major enquired.

"Jenny is my little sister. I found her wandering along the riverbank two years ago when she was only three years old. At least I think she was three."

This reply took the Major completely by surprise. "What about her parents, where are they?"

"Don't rightly know, Sir. Her mother either died or deserted her, I expect. After I found Jenny, I went back to the place every day for a whole month, just in case her mum had lost her, but no one wanted her. God sent her to me and now she is my little sister."

Her answer sent cold shivers down the Major's spine, and he found himself wondering why this little girl appeared so different from others her age.

"How old are you, Liza?"

"I'm twelve years old on December tenth, Sir."

"Are you expecting me to believe that you live alone, that you have been taking care of another little girl for the past two years on your own, and you are only eleven years old?"

Robert appeared annoyed by Liza's story and sternly assured the Major, "Told you, Sir, these little mudlarks live in dishonesty. I wouldn't trust what she says; it's only another way to beg for more money."

Liza glared at the driver, her blue eyes clouded. It seemed as if she felt hurt by Robert's remarks and resented his slur regarding her honesty.

The Major disagreed with Robert's cynical views and sympathized with the little girl's plight. He was moved to compassion by the horrendous conditions of her life, "Please take back your candlestick, I really don't want it."

"But, Sir, you bought it, and it really is a nice candlestick," begged Liza.

The Major reassured her, "It is alright, child, you may keep the money."

Even though his heart went out to her, he found it very difficult to believe that such a young girl had actually cared for a younger child for the past two years without adult help or supervision. Perhaps Robert was correct in thinking that her story was a ruse to get more money. Suddenly, the Major felt truly grateful to God that his own children weren't in the same predicament as Liza, whatever that might actually be.

# Chapter 2

# Laura's Reaction

*A*fter he returned home to his mansion, the Major enjoyed a delightful evening meal with his family. Then he took his six-year-old granddaughter, Pamela, and his grandson, James, who was four, over to the stables to see the horses. Pamela was especially interested in the horses since her parents had promised her a pony for her upcoming birthday. They visited each stall, offering small handfuls of hay to the horses and ponies while the grooms went about their business of watering and brushing the animals. Pointing to the Major's splendid white stallion, Pamela announced, "That's my favourite."

"I'm afraid he's a little too much horse for you, just yet, young lady," said the Major. "Perhaps some day when you're a little older you will be able to manage him. Just now, you should be looking at something more like one of these ponies. What do you say if we go back now, and see if we can find us something hot to drink?"

\* \* \*

Later that evening as they prepared for bed, the Major told his wife, Laura, all about his encounter with the little orphan girl and the unbelievable story she had told about taking care of another homeless youngster for the past two years.

Laura sat at her dressing table, and then said in a voice more aggrieved than dismayed. "Never have I heard such a story in all my life. I wonder where their parents are?"

"I asked her that very same question," the Major replied, "and she told me her parents were in heaven. She didn't say much about the other child except that she found her two years ago, that she had tried in vain to find the child's mother and that she has looked after her ever since."

"That certainly is an unusual story. Perhaps Robert is correct that the girl was just trying to look for pity so that it would be easier to sell whatever it was she was selling."

"I really don't think so, Laura. I can't explain why but when I looked into her clear blue eyes, I just knew she was honest; and the way she spoke up to Robert was not like your average eleven year old."

"You surprise me, David, I've never seen you so upset over a little street urchin. You know, dear, the vicar and his wife are coming for tea tomorrow. Why don't you tell them about your encounter with the child? I'm certain they will know more about what should be done than we do. Now why don't you forget all about street orphans and go to sleep?"

The Major marvelled that Laura could be so matter-of-fact about the children's situation and that she hadn't been more sympathetic toward them. He had noticed lately that Laura appeared to have lost some of her gentler feelings of caring and compassion that she had displayed when she was younger. Not for the first time, whiffs of guilt entered his head, prompting him to wonder if his career in the army had been the cause of their losing the beautiful feelings of love they had once shared.

For the next two hours the Major lay awake as he wondered how he and Laura could recapture their lost love and affection. It was becoming more and more apparent to him every day just how much they had drifted apart.

* * *

The following morning during breakfast, Laura and the Major watched the heavy rain beating on the stone walks and dashing against the windowpanes as the blustery wind threw itself at everything in its path. They agreed that the weather was more typical of late November.

As the Major listened to the pounding rain and looked around his snug and warm dining room with its oak panelling and its highly polished floors covered with Persian rugs, his thoughts settled on his family. Waves of gratitude for having such a beautiful wife and two wonderful children swept over him. Such emotions were virtually unknown to the Major. Then he realized it was only since he had met the little street orphan, a child who, in his opinion, had so little to be grateful for, that such feelings of gratefulness had emerged.

Laura and the Major spent the early part of the day in the parlour, contentedly reading by the fire as the rain continued to beat down, saturating the ground, turning roads treacherous with mud and creating a small, temporary lake in the lower meadow.

At two o'clock, the maid announced that the vicar and his wife had arrived and then she ushered them into the parlour. After the formalities of welcoming the guests had been completed, Laura rang for tea, which was served along with the usual topics of conversation. The Major found it all singularly dull—refurbishing the church; the following year's planned congregational events, including picnics and outings; the need to help the poor; and how they were chronically short of funds.

"Speaking of the poor," Laura interjected, "David had the most extraordinary experience yesterday." She then related to the vicar and his wife her husband's entire experience of the day before— how and where he had met a little street urchin who tried to sell her candleholder to him, and her claim of caring for a little sister on her own.

The vicar sat up straight and stiff in his chair. "That must have been a rather frightening experience for you! I believe there are many children living in the streets of London; in fact I have heard them referred to as little guttersnipes by those who have to deal with them. I just can't imagine how we have all this poverty; after all this is England, 1834, and we are supposed to be a civilized country."

"But what do you think might be done to help them?" asked the Major. "Surely there must be somewhere they could be cared for!"

The vicar's wife responded, "There are workhouses that would probably take the older girl but the other child is too young and she could be quite a problem. She should really be sent to an orphanage."

The very thought of putting a child in the workhouse appalled the Major, and he remarked, "I hear that they work the children ten hours a day just for their food."

The vicar stated that in his parish he was not used to such problems and felt quite inadequate to handle such a task, but that he would see what could be done.

The Major then explained to the vicar and his

wife that the child had opened his eyes to some feelings he had not experienced for some time.

"I tell you, Vicar, if you could have seen how joyful she was when she had her candlestick returned and was still allowed to keep the two pence. It was an inspiring feeling. I felt it was good for my soul.

"Until witnessing that child's behaviour yesterday, I couldn't have imagined anyone getting so much pleasure out of an old two-penny candlestick. And yet I keep wondering if she was as genuine in her display of joy as she appeared to be. If so, she must have an extraordinarily positive outlook on life and I'd love to know where it comes from."

The vicar smiled pompously. "It appears to me, Major, you must have had some kind of inspirational revelation. You know, the Good Book tells us that appreciation is a wonderful thing."

Laura quickly agreed with the vicar, then went on to explain, "Our coachman felt certain the child was just putting on a show to appeal to David's sympathy."

The vicar immediately responded, "I have heard it said that around the waterfront area some beggars are very proficient at their craft. Perhaps it is true that the girl was performing for your benefit, Major Rutherford."

The more the Major listened to the conversation, the more it became apparent to him that nobody really cared enough about the child to give her the benefit of the doubt or even to look into the truthfulness of her story. Gradually the talk reverted to the financial needs of the parish and how much Major Rutherford could be counted on to donate. After a sip of port wine and the Major's promise of a substantial donation, the vicar and his wife departed.

Once their guests had taken their leave, Laura challenged the Major, "I have never seen you so obsessed about anything as you are with those two little urchins. I suggest you just forget them for a while. After all, we can't be responsible for every stray in London."

# Chapter 3

# Returning to the Bridge

$\mathcal{T}$he more the Major thought about it, the more he knew in his heart that he had to return to talk to the child, Liza.

One week later, following an appointment at his club, the Major instructed Robert to drive him to the place where they had first met the little street urchin. When they arrived at the spot, Robert drove up and down the street for the greater part of twenty minutes, but to the Major's disappointment, they saw no sign of the child.

"Maybe the girl doesn't live around these parts, Sir. It's possible she could live anywhere in London."

"All right, Robert, you may as well take me home," the Major sighed.

Five minutes later Robert stopped the carriage. "There she is, Sir, over there, down by the wall."

"I see her. Drive over! I want to talk with her."

As the carriage approached, Liza appeared a little nervous until she recognized the Major and greeted him with a warm smile and a curtsy. "Good afternoon, Sir."

"Good afternoon, Liza. How are you?"

"Very well, thank you, Sir."

"And your little sister, Jenny, how is she doing?"

"Not so well, sir. She is very poorly, she has a very bad cold." The words were no sooner out of her mouth than she began to cough uncontrollably herself.

"Do you live nearby, Liza?"

"Yes, Sir, just over there."

"Can you show us where you stay?" Robert asked suspiciously.

Liza stared at the Major, then at Robert. "That way," she said, pointing down a street lined with old, derelict buildings.

The Major dismounted from the carriage and asked Robert to wait for him, "I want to see where she lives." As they walked off, the Major tried to reassure Liza that he hoped to be able to help Jenny.

At first the streets were very busy and they had

to dodge horses and carts rumbling over the old cobblestones and weave their way through foot traffic, but soon the streets became narrow lanes and dark alleyways with fewer and fewer people in sight. Major Rutherford started to feel a little uneasy about the district and the appearance of some of the local residents.

"Just a minute, Liza, how much farther is it to where you live?" the Major asked.

Pointing her finger she replied, "Not far, Sir, just over there."

"You said that some minutes ago."

She directed her blue gaze straight into Major Rutherford's eyes and asked, "Are you afraid?"

"To be quite truthful with you, young lady, I don't feel at all secure in this neighbourhood."

With a smile on her face, Liza offered the Major her hand, saying, "As long as you hold my hand you will be safe."

Her words took the Major by surprise. He thought to himself: *What an unusual remark for such a small child to make; it should be the adult who reassures the child. I can't imagine why I'd be safer holding her hand.* Regardless of his thoughts, he clasped her hand and continued to follow along.

After another twenty steps, the strongest feeling came over him that he was being led to evil deeds. He quickly released her hand and at the same time wondered to himself: *Was Robert correct all along about our young street urchin playacting?* Within a split second of letting go of her hand, he turned to question her but she was gone. It was as if she had simply vanished into thin air.

The Major hurriedly retraced his steps, and as he approached the carriage, Robert let out a great sigh of relief, pleased to find that the Major had returned unscathed from his adventure into the backstreets. Then, after the Major had recounted a brief description of the events, Robert felt a little smug that he had been justified in his opinion of the child, thinking that perhaps now the Major would come to his senses and see the little gutter-snipe for what she really was.

All the way home, the Major couldn't get the child out of his mind and repeatedly asked himself if he may have overreacted. Perhaps the child was telling the truth.

# Chapter 4

# Meeting Jenny

$\mathcal{T}$he following morning over breakfast, the Major discussed with Laura his experience of the previous afternoon. "You would be appalled by the living conditions in that area, Laura. Liza claimed that many people live in abandoned buildings, and I saw with my own eyes people apparently making their homes in any number of decrepit hovels. It's absolutely deplorable that any small child should have to live in such poverty."

With a tone of haughty self-righteousness, Laura remarked, "When you think about it, dear, there have to be some poor so that there can be some rich, and we should be grateful that we are the rich."

Laura's callous words and indifferent manner surprised the Major. It was obvious that she had missed his point.

"Perhaps that's the problem, my dear. We say we appreciate our affluent life, but we don't feel it or show it. Tell me, Laura, how long is it since you honestly felt grateful for what you have and how you live?"

With a hint of annoyance in her voice, Laura replied, "I really don't understand your question, dear. I've always been grateful for what we have!"

It was clear to the Major that, indeed, Laura didn't understand what he was feeling. He remembered when he first met Laura; she had been not only the most beautiful but also the most caring and compassionate person he had ever known. Often he wondered what had happened to change her so much. Deep in his heart he hoped that some day the lost feelings that Laura had once displayed to him would return.

\* \* \*

Weeks went by, and by the time of October's passing everyone had forgotten all about the encounter with the little street urchin. The icy, finger-numbing winds of November brought with them more torrential rain. The estate agent and farm hands were busily preparing the barn and stables for the winter, ensuring that Major Rutherford's animals would have warm, dry quarters. In the first stall was a very important young filly the Major had bought for his grand-daughter Pamela's birthday, which was now only one day away. The Major stopped by to speak with the head groom, then visited the pony to see how she was getting on, as she had arrived at his stables only a few days earlier. She was a beautiful little animal, gracefully proportioned, a rich chestnut colour with a white blaze on her fore-head. When he approached, she raised her head and eyed him cautiously, then nickered gently as though welcoming an old friend. He felt assured that she was settling in nicely.

The following morning, the sun appeared as if to celebrate Pamela's special day and the house was a bustle of activity as the servants prepared for the day's festivities. Overseeing the preparations in the kitchen was a joyful, buxom woman who had been the family cook for the past twenty years, and who was affectionately known as Cookie by the staff and the children of the house. She had spent much of the morning making a beautiful birthday cake for the occasion.

In the afternoon, the entire family, plus the numerous children who constituted Pamela's circle of friends, gathered together for her party. The cake was appreciated by all and the gift of the little chestnut-coloured filly was an overwhelming success. The Major and Laura watched as the children played and rode the new filly, which by now had been named Lady.

But amidst the gaiety of Pamela's party with all the happy young faces, the Major somehow had troubling memories of the little street urchin, and doubts started to enter his mind. He recalled the feelings of fear and apprehension he had suffered when Liza had taken him to see her little sister, Jenny, and he wondered whether he had misjudged the child and her intentions. He asked himself again if there even was such a person as Jenny.

Perhaps it was his army training that had taught him that once you take on a job, you finish it—and one way or another the Major was determined to discover the truth about Liza and her little "sister." Early the following morning the skies were clear and it looked like it would be another sunny day, so he saddled the grey mare and rode toward London Bridge, hoping to find the place where he had first come across the urchin. From there it would only be a couple of minutes' ride to where he last saw the child.

On arriving at the place he recognized as the site of their first meeting, he headed toward the street along which Liza had led him. What he first took to be bundles of rags and cast-off clothing in many doorways turned out, as he drew closer, to be sleeping people. Some were so meagrely dressed that he wondered how they could survive the nights with so little shelter. There was an uneasy feeling to the place; as a matter of fact, it reminded

Major Rutherford of many places he had been in India where people would slit your throat for a sixpence. Finally he came upon the spot where they had parted, but there was no sign of the child. Determined to find her, he asked an elderly man passing by if he knew a young girl named Liza who lived somewhere close by.

"What's it to ye?" he snapped.

"She has a little sister who may be sick and I'd like to help her if I possibly can."

"Are ye a doctor or sumfing?" the old man asked suspiciously.

"No, I'm not a doctor. I'm just a friend."

"You must be right rich to have an 'orse like that," the man growled.

Ignoring his comment, the Major repeated, "Do you know such a girl?"

"There's plenty young gels about! What's she look like?"

The Major described Liza briefly, "She's a bright little thing, blond hair, blue eyes, about eleven years old, but mature for her age."

"Do ye have any money? Could ye spare a penny fer a poor soul like me?"

The old man looked like he hadn't had a good meal for weeks. Bending down toward him, the Major handed him two pennies, suggesting he get himself a meal.

"Thank ye kindly, Sir, ye're a kind gentleman, ye are, but I haven't 'eard of a wench in these parts that fits them descriptions." And with these words he hurried away.

A young woman carrying a squirming baby approached the Major and asked, "You looking fer someone special, Mister, or can I help?"

"Yes, I'm looking for someone who might live in this neighbourhood, a little girl called Liza." He told her the same story he had told the old man and described Liza's appearance and the clothing he had last seen her wearing.

"Can't rightly say, Sir, could be any one of the dozens of little blighters that lives in these parts. I can't say as I ever seen 'er."

Doubts that Liza even lived in the neighbourhood flooded the Major's head, but just as he was about to head home he heard a gentle voice calling, "Sir?" Turning, he saw Liza.

He dismounted and approached her, explaining that since their last meeting he had often wondered what had happened to her. "It was as if you had just vanished."

Dropping her head Liza said that she had felt there was a lot of distrust in his heart and that he had doubted her word. "When I offered you my hand for safety, again you lacked faith in me."

The Major couldn't believe what the girl was saying. That she was talking to him in such a manner astounded him, but before he could respond Liza continued, "It was nice of you to show such concern and caring for me and Jenny. Now I feel I can trust you. You have kind eyes; my mum had kind eyes. She always talked about people's eyes.

She used to tell me that our eyes are the windows to our soul."

"I'm afraid, Liza, I have little idea of what you are trying to say," the Major replied. Then noticing how lightly she was dressed, "Aren't you cold wearing that thin shawl at this time of year?"

"This is my favourite shawl! It belonged to my mum and it helps me to keep warm. And it's so pretty."

The fact that the child could express joy at the beauty of her threadbare shawl as she stood shivering in the biting wind astonished the Major. It was difficult for him to comprehend her attitude under such conditions, and waves of gratitude flowed though every vein in his body as he realized just how kind life had been to him.

"How is your little sister Jenny?"

"Much better now. Her sickness is almost gone. Many people around here died with the same sickness, but Jenny and me, we prayed, and God made her all better."

The sky had clouded over as the Major and Liza talked, and soon a fine drizzle started. The poor child looked so cold the Major asked her if she would like to join him for some hot food. Liza stood with a shy look on her face as she debated whether or not to go with him, but the very thought of hot food was irresistible to her.

"Yes, Sir, I'd be grateful."

"Why don't we fetch Jenny and take her along with us?"

"Well, Sir, I don't think Jenny is well enough to join us. When I left her she was sleeping and usually Jenny sleeps for hours."

Doubts and suspicions again made the Major wonder if Liza was making excuses about a sister she never had as a ploy to gain more for her efforts.

They walked to the nearest inn and inquired about the possibility of obtaining a hot meal. The bustling innkeeper said he had nothing left but chicken, but he could provide them with that and some bread and cheese. "Oh, Sir, chicken is my favourite," said Liza.

Never had the Major seen a child her age eat so much. When she was finished, she started to pick over the remains and put pieces of food in a cloth she carried in her dress pocket. Observing that the Major had noticed her actions, she sheepishly remarked, "This is for Jenny."

He nodded sympathetically as she collected every last scrap of food. Major Rutherford settled with the landlord and he and Liza left the inn and returned to the street. The rain had finally stopped but streams of water still ran over the cobblestones.

"Come, Liza, jump up behind me on my horse and I'll take you home."

Following Liza's directions, the Major soon found himself in a narrow street lined with time-worn houses and abandoned buildings. Pointing to a ramshackle old building, Liza announced, "That is where I live."

"Where?" the Major asked, looking around incredulously as Liza slid off the horse.

"Over there." Just as she said that a little girl, pale faced, redheaded and dressed in a collection of hand-me-down clothing, came skipping out of the condemned building and gave Liza a big hug.

"Jenny, this is the man I told you about, the one who bought our candlestick."

The Major was impressed by the little one's manners as she curtsied, "Pleased to meet you, Sir."

Liza invited the Major into the cellar of the dilapidated house she and her sister called home. It had a single room with an uneven stone floor and a pocket-sized window high up on the wall that let in little light but plenty of cold air. The tiny room was surprisingly clean but very chilly. The furnishings were sparse—an old table, two straight-backed wooden chairs and one padded armchair. On the table sat a candleholder with a half-burnt candle. Next to it, but safely against the wall, rested a delicate music box with a miniature ballerina gracefully posed on top. The mantle above the fireplace held the candlestick Liza had tried to sell to the Major. In front of the fireplace was a scrap of torn rug and in the corner were two beds made up with a single blanket each. The room smelled musty and damp.

Liza brought out the cloth containing the food from the inn and spread it before Jenny, who started to eat it as if she hadn't seen such astonishing riches for some time.

Liza invited the Major to take a seat in the old padded chair in front of the fireplace. The tiny fire it contained was barely large enough to heat a pot of water.

"Jenny and me, we don't get many visitors; would you like a cup of tea, Sir? We have lots of tea."

"No thank you, Liza. I think I've had quite sufficient for now."

"My mum always said it was good manners to give guests a cup of tea."

"Your mum must have been a wonderful person, Liza. What happened to her?"

"She died three years ago with a very big cold in her chest. I think the doctor said it was consumption or some name like that."

"May I ask about your father, Liza, what happened to him?"

"My dad was killed in an accident down a coal mine when I was five."

"What about your grandparents? Do they know where you are?"

"My mum told me that my grandma and granddad told her never to come back to their house if she married my dad."

Shocked by her story, the Major asked her if she knew why her grandfather and grandmother would say such a thing.

"Something to do with my granddad and grandma being posh and my dad wasn't.

"My mum and dad had a wonderful life together; our house was always full of love and happy times. They loved each other and Mum was always acting funny and Dad and me would laugh.

"When my dad died, Mum and me went back home to Granddad and Grandma's for help but they told us to go away and that they wanted nothing to do with us, so we found a little place in George Street. Then, after my mum went to heaven I found this place on my own. Nobody was using it so I stayed here."

Little Jenny finished every scrap of her meal then beamed at the Major. "That was the best food I've had in all my life. It's just like a party, isn't it Liza," she declared, and snuggled closer to the fire, rubbing herself as if she were trying to keep warm.

Major Rutherford thought to himself how ghastly it was for two small children to live under such conditions, yet they appeared happier than most he knew within his circle of friends. For the world, he couldn't see the remotest chance of himself or any of his friends saying that they would be happy under such dreadful circumstances. The Major was lost for words and had no idea how to communicate with these children, especially when Liza started to tell him with great pride about her possessions she had inherited from her mother and how grateful both she and Jenny felt at having a place of their own.

The Major was astounded by how little it took to please the two youngsters: a few meagre possessions and a spartan shelter. He recalled his experience in India where the poverty and living conditions were often pathetic, yet many of the people appeared happier than he was, even though he was an officer in His Majesty's army. For many years he had been fascinated by this situation and had tried in vain to figure out what makes poor people happy under such vile circumstances while many wealthy people can be unhappy with ideal living conditions.

Little Jenny stood up and went over to her bed where she retrieved a little rag doll. With great pride she showed it to the Major, told him that its name was Molly, and then said, "I'm taking Molly over to the fire to keep her warm."

As she said this, a particularly strong gust of harsh November wind blew under the ill-fitting door and reached across the floor toward the fire where the children huddled to keep warm.

When the Major had been abroad in the army, the poverty he had seen hadn't concerned him, but there was something about the plight of Liza and her little sister that was different, making him feel obligated to help them in some way. Perhaps his conscience was starting to bother him, since he had so much in life while they had so little.

Informing Liza that he had to go but would be back to see her and her little sister again, he handed her a six-penny piece.

Liza, amazed at the thought of being given so much money, immediately responded, "Sir, I can't take all that money. Mum and Dad always said it just wasn't right to accept money without earning it.

They always said that if I had enough faith God would take care of me."

With the greatest admiration the Major listened intently to the child's words, then answered, "That's a nice way to look at it, Liza, so why don't you accept my gift as if it were God helping you and your little sister? Please, Liza, it would make me feel good if you would accept this money and buy some food for you and Jenny."

Liza then said, "It was God that sent you to Jenny and me—for a purpose. I knew the first time we met that you were sent to help me with Jenny."

Surprised by her remark, the Major asked, "How did you know that God sent me?"

"Because I know these things. It was meant to be that you help me with Jenny."

The Major stood absolutely flabbergasted by what he was hearing. "But how could you be so sure that I was sent to help you with Jenny?"

"When Jenny was sick I prayed for a guardian angel and that day you were sent to me. That was the day you bought my candlestick."

"Liza, just because I bought your candlestick doesn't make me a guardian angel."

With the most beautiful smile Liza said, "My mum said guardian angels come in lots of different shapes and sizes."

Secretly the Major was pleased at the thought of Liza calling him a guardian angel, though he knew better than to call himself one.

Finally, Liza reluctantly accepted the money and, just as the Major was leaving, little Jenny came over and gave him a big hug, kissed him on the cheek and thanked him for the food.

Her action brought tears to his eyes while his mind scrambled to ascertain what was happening to him and why he was having such unusual feelings of gratitude toward life.

# Chapter 5

# Cookie

That evening, the Major discussed the children's situation with Laura. "The reactions of those two children to the slightest kindness made me experience overwhelming feelings of appreciation for the life I've been given, feelings I've never had before. Tell me, Laura, can you suggest any way we might be able to help Liza and her sister?"

Laura displayed an air of indifference. "Why are you suddenly so interested in two stray orphans? What possible difference could it make to you how they live?"

"I can't explain it, Laura, but there's something special about the older one, Liza. The way she accepts life without complaint fascinates me.

"There's something about the way the child talks. I tell you, my dear, never have I felt this way. She has opened my eyes to a new way of seeing life."

"Come dear, let's not exaggerate what the child may have done," Laura cautioned.

"It's something I can't explain intellectually; it's more of a good feeling. It's as if I'm seeing life for the first time—since I met that young street urchin my life hasn't been the same."

Laura didn't know how to answer her husband's words, other than to say sharply, "I haven't any idea what in heaven's name you are talking about."

Although it had nothing to do with what they were talking about, Laura began to feel the way she did when she thought about the Major's time in the military. Laura couldn't forgive the Major for being in the army and always felt that their marriage was secondary to him. Being a soldier's wife had never appealed to her and she had always been jealous of all the time he devoted to the army instead of her. And now he was beginning to spend more and more time on these two little street urchins. It was like the army all over again.

The Major wasn't surprised by her uncaring remarks and he knew Laura didn't understand his feelings. How could she when he didn't understand them himself?

In an effort to put an end to the conversation, Laura finally suggested that he get in touch with the vicar again to see if he could offer a solution to the dilemma of the two young orphans.

The following afternoon the Major went to talk with the vicar. But when he arrived at the vicarage, he was informed by the vicar's wife that her husband had a fundraising campaign to organize and wouldn't be back for several hours.

"Is there anything I can help you with?" she asked.

The Major again described the children's situation to her, finishing with the hope that she might be able to offer some solution to the problem. The vicar's wife explained that both she and her husband had asked a few people about the problem, but other than the workhouse for the elder of the two children they hadn't been able to come up with any suitable solutions. "As far as the smaller one is concerned, we have no idea what can be done about her, but we will certainly keep our eyes open. Sometimes if a child is lucky, someone can be found to take it in," she said, as though she were speaking about a stray dog.

The Major felt frustrated that nobody seemed to take the situation of Liza and her little sister very seriously. He thanked the vicar's wife for her time and left as soon as politeness would allow.

On the ride home, the Major couldn't get Liza and her little sister out of his mind. Then he remembered that if any of his own children had wanted comforting when Laura and he were not available, they wouldn't go to their nanny, they would go to the cook, Mrs. Smith. Cookie, as she was known throughout the household, had a warm and loving nature, and a good helping of common sense. That evening after supper the Major asked the cook into his study and explained the children's situation to her.

Cookie sat silent for the longest time, and then she finally replied, "It just ain't right that them little ones should live like that, but I have no idea how I could possibly help you, Sir. But I'll certainly keep my ears open and maybe we can find someone that will take care of the poor little mites.

"In the meantime we could send them some food, Sir."

"Splendid idea, Mrs. Smith. The next time I go to see them you can make up a picnic basket. As a matter of fact, if I remember correctly, the elder of the two will soon have a birthday and I could take it tomorrow."

\* \* \*

The next day the wind blew with special ferocity and the temperature dropped to below freezing; icicles hung from the eaves and the windowsills shone like sparkling diamonds.

After finishing her breakfast duties for the family, and before becoming involved with lunch preparations, Cookie filled a picnic basket with all sorts of delicious treats for the children. She included chicken, bread, winter pears, thick, nourishing soup and sweets, all of which the Major had previously approved. Then she handed Robert a used but warm coat for each of the children and two pairs of used shoes, saying, "These are too small for my son's children and I thought the little mites could get some use from them."

At this point, the maid included two pairs of used gloves.

Robert said nothing as Cookie packed the food for the children. Finally, his pessimistic outlook on life showed itself as he snarled at Cookie, "Spoiling the little beggars, I'd say. Giving them meat ain't healthy for them. Their stomachs ain't used to it and it can drive them mad in the head."

Shocked by his words, Cookie asked him, "Who told you such rubbish?"

"It was one of them posh doctors at the Major's club. I overheard him talking to one of his colleagues and he said meat can drive some poor people mad in the head and the best thing for them is bread and milk."

The Major came in to check on the preparations, and then Laura made an unexpected entrance carrying two blankets and two pillows, saying she hoped they would be of use to the children.

Overwhelmed with pleasure by Laura's change of heart toward the children, the Major smiled broadly. Then Laura suggested it might be better if Robert delivered the gifts to the children by himself. "It's such a dreadful day, my dear, I wonder if you shouldn't stay at home."

"I'm afraid, Laura, this is something I have to

do. There's something so unusual about that child, and whatever it is, I want to discover it for myself."

Within minutes, Robert had pulled the carriage outside the kitchen door and loaded all the food and gifts. An icy rain began falling as the temperature continued to drop, and the Major couldn't help but wonder how the children were managing in such bone-chilling weather.

When the Major stuck his head out of the carriage window to guide Robert toward the children's home, the relentless rain bit into his skin like tiny razor cuts, making him realize the uncomfortable situation Robert was in when driving in such dreadful weather.

It was around one in the afternoon when they arrived. Robert dismounted from the carriage and knocked on the door where the children lived, but there was no answer.

"Nobody home, Sir."

"Try again," the Major demanded.

The second time Robert knocked, Liza cautiously answered the door and not recognizing him asked, "What do you want?"

Robert pointed to the carriage, "Beg your pardon, Miss, but the Major would like to call on you."

The moment Liza saw who it was she broke into a lovely smile and called little Jenny. As usual the room was cold and damp. Robert started to unload all the gifts, which almost overwhelmed the children. Robert stood at the doorway in silence as the children joyfully sprang to unpack their bounty, then he said, "Beg your pardon, Sir, with your permission I would like to return to the carriage."

"By all means, Robert, I won't be long."

Little Jenny spotted the pound cake that Cookie had made for the special occasion and asked Liza if she could have a piece. Liza sliced the cake into pieces and asked the Major, "Would you like a cup of tea and a piece of cake, sir?"

"I would love to join you in a cup of tea, but I won't have any cake," he said, not wanting to deprive the children of even a morsel of their treats.

While they waited for the kettle to boil, the children huddled near the tiny flames, trying to keep warm. With such a dismally small fire the kettle seemed to take forever to boil. Finally, the kettle began to sing and Liza made the tea. She poured it into two chipped china cups and a small crockery bowl, then passed 'round the cake.

Liza didn't look too well and regularly turned her head aside to cough, an incessant, wracking cough that seemed to come from deep within her lungs.

"Perhaps it would be advisable for you to see a doctor, Liza," said the Major. "Your cough sounds quite bad to me and if you want I will have my doctor examine you and Jenny."

"I'm sure this little cold will soon go away," Liza replied, not wanting to embarrass her new friend by pointing out that doctors charged more for their services than she could make in a month's hard work.

There was a knock at the door and to the Major's amazement it was Robert showing his softer side. He carried three canvas bags filled with chopped wood, which he had placed in the back of the carriage before leaving the house. Stacking most of the wood beside the fireplace, he then built up the fire and within minutes it was blazing cheerily and the little room was comfortably warm.

"Oh, thank you, Sir!" Liza exclaimed, and then asked Robert if he would like a piece of cake and some tea.

Robert hesitated and looked over at the Major, as if to ask permission. The Major picked up Robert's concern. "Yes, Robert, why don't you join the party?" he invited.

The visit lasted about an hour, and then little Jenny, her stomach filled with cake, fell sound asleep. The major watched Liza help Jenny to bed and once again wondered how it was that Liza could be so happy with her life under such appalling conditions. He asked Liza why she always appeared so happy with her life.

Liza replied, "My mum always said 'Happiness comes from our hearts, and if we can keep our hearts and heads full of nice thoughts we will always live in contentment.'"

Liza's words surprised the Major and he wondered what kind of woman this child's mother had been, to think in such a manner.

"It sounds like you loved your mum."

"Yes Sir, she was a very gentle person who helped lots of people until she went to heaven. Some people used to call my mum an angel."

"In what way did she help others?" asked the Major.

Liza thought for a while before answering his question. "Sometimes she would sit all night with people who were sick and talk to them about God and that would help them. When people were sad and unhappy, my mum would explain to them how sometimes it was only their own thoughts that were making them unhappy and if they could understand what she was saying, it would help make them feel well."

"Your mother must have been hurt by your granddad and grandma refusing to help her when she was in need." And to himself he thought that the fact that they wouldn't make peace and forget old wounds was rather petty under the circumstances.

"My mum told me she felt sorry for them not allowing themselves to know my daddy and me. She said they were lost and weren't thinking right, and they just didn't know any better.

"My mum often said, 'We have to learn to forgive people who don't understand.'"

"That was very Christian of your mother to think that way, Liza. Many people I know would have been hurt and resentful in such a situation.

Tell me, have you been in contact with your grandfather or grandmother since you lost your mother?"

"No, Sir, I felt it would be better if I stayed alone. Sometimes I'd think about going to see them, but then I'd wonder if they would ever accept Jenny, and I would never want to be separated from my little sister."

"With your permission, Liza, I would willingly contact your grandparents and talk with them."

"No, all I want is a nice home for Jenny and I know in my heart that it will happen soon."

"My dear child, you don't understand—your grandparents should be contacted. After all, they do have some responsibility in this situation."

Liza looked at the Major, paused, and then said with overwhelming certainty, "Soon Jenny will find her new home. Then I will talk to my granddad and grandma."

Never had the Major heard any child, or adult for that matter, talk with such assurance. "How can you be so certain?" he asked.

"Because I know," she replied, not in an arrogant way, but as if it had already been arranged.

The time came to depart and so the Major and Robert said their goodbyes. When they left, the fire was ablaze and the entire room was cosy and warm. Once outside, Robert and the Major agreed that it was a satisfying feeling to know the children had plenty of food in their little stomachs, a warm fire and enough firewood for a few days.

As the Major climbed into the carriage, Robert apologized for his behaviour and his previous misjudgement of Liza.

"I'm afraid, Robert, we are both guilty of misjudging the poor child, but let's not dwell on our mistakes. Instead, let us see how you and I can help the children."

# Chapter 6

# Laura's Awakening

To the Major's delight, Laura was more than pleased to hear about the success of the mission with the children and to know that the presents had been so well appreciated. The Major had always stood in awe of Laura's beauty and admired the elegant way she had matured. And now, as Laura softened her attitude toward helping the children, the effect of this showed in her face, revealing a renewed gentleness that was very apparent to him.

There was a general softening of her appearance, and small lines of irritation and frustration seemed to be melting away. Even the way she stood seemed less stiff and irritated.

That evening was one they would never forget, as Laura asked for details of the Major's visit with the youngsters and shared his enthusiasm in looking for possible means of easing their lives.

The following morning at breakfast, Laura explained how the conversation of the previous evening had made her do some soul searching on gratefulness. "I have just realized that, like many others, I have been taking my luxurious life for granted. I simply never realized how easy it was to slip into feelings of indifference for those who are less fortunate."

The Major realised that, in all the years they had been married, this was the first time he had heard Laura talk with such empathy or concern for others.

With tears in her eyes, Laura remarked that the young strays were affecting her as they did him. Then she noted that not only Cookie but the entire household staff was involved in trying to ease the plight of the children.

Then, with deep tenderness in her voice, Laura asked the Major to tell her more about the children and what he found so special about them.

"There's definitely something unique about the way those two children appreciate the smallest things. And the way they talk and act is not a normal, childlike way. For example, when I asked Liza why she was always so happy, do you know what she replied? She said her mum told her that 'Happy thoughts bring happy days and sad thoughts bring sad days.' I tell you, Laura, there's a beautiful simplicity to her mother's words and when Liza quoted those words, something in me stirred.

"I could see that you and I had drifted apart because of all the stress of military life, with my being away much of the time. When I retired from the military I thought we would somehow work out our differences and renew some of the old feelings we used to have for each other.

"Now I can see clearly that all those old wounds in our marriage were yesterday's problems, so why don't we start anew? Let's take the little mudlark's advice and try to forgive each other for anything done or said in the past and try to rekindle the old love we had for each other."

Laura stood up from the table, threw her arms around the Major's neck and began to weep.

When she had recovered her composure, she said, "My dear, you have no idea how delighted I am to hear you say those words. Why don't we go on a voyage somewhere, just you and I and get to know each other all over again?"

"Splendid idea, Laura, splendid! Have you any idea where you'd like to go?"

"Yes, I'd love to see all the wonders of Greece. Imagine seeing the Parthenon for ourselves, and maybe I could try some watercolours. I've heard the sea is such a brilliant shade of blue that it rivals the sky. Just sitting in the sun together would be such a treat. Oh! Let's do it, David, it will be such fun."

"I've always wanted to see Greece," he replied. "Once we figure out where and when we want to go, I'll make the necessary arrangements. I imagine February would be a good time to sail away from our bitterly cold English weather."

Although Christmas was still some weeks away, Laura was enthusiastic at the thought of going on such a vacation and exhibited the most beautiful smile, saying, "What a superb Christmas gift for both of us. Isn't it a wonderful feeling to see our lives coming together again? And have you noticed how everyone in the household appears to be in a very pleasant mood these days?"

"I don't know about the rest of the servants, but Robert appears to be a new man. I couldn't believe the empathy he exhibited for the children. I'm seeing a different side of him every day and most definitely for the better!"

* * *

Weeks later, Laura was still filled with excitement over their proposed trip. There was so much to be done. She had countless fittings with her dressmaker and long conferences with her friends deciding what to take and what to leave behind. But even with all these extra preparations and everything that had to be done to get ready for Christmas, she noticed that all she heard about in the house was Liza and her little sister. She mentioned it to the Major, and then said, "Just this morning I went down to the kitchen to talk to the cook, and both she and the maid were in a very jovial mood talking about the children. The more I hear about this Liza, the more intriguing she becomes. Some day I must meet her in person."

"You will, and when you do, you will see what I mean. She is a very wise young lady, far beyond her years. At times the way she looks at me makes even me feel quite insecure. I know it sounds rather absurd, but it's as if she knows what I'm thinking. I know that she knew we were having problems in our marriage, and yet I said not one word to her about our personal life."

Laura was stunned by her husband's remark. "What makes you believe such a thing? That is simply impossible for anyone to know!"

"That's what I thought, but I can assure you she did know," the Major replied.

"Robert and I visited her again recently, and at that time she told us how her mother had taught her to forgive those who had harmed her in the past. Believe it or not, this eleven-year-old child started to explain to Robert how he lacked trust and faith and how this had a lot to do with his being so unhappy."

Laura smiled at that and asked, "And what was Robert's reaction to Liza's observation?"

"Surprisingly, he didn't say a word, but just stood there with a shocked expression on his face!"

"What else did this little urchin speak of?"

"Well, for instance, she explained to Robert and me the benefits of being grateful for even the small things in life. Both Robert and I were dumbfounded by her words. Here I am, a wealthy man and unhappy, yet this little girl, who has so little, appears satisfied with her entire life. Again I had to ask myself, what are the secret ingredients that make people such as Liza and her little sister so content with life?

"Curiosity got the better of me so again I asked Liza why she was so pleased with her life. This is how she answered, 'Sir, may I be so bold as to suggest to you that perhaps you are looking in the wrong place for your happiness. My mum always said that all the wealth in the world could never buy you happiness and that happiness can only be found from your own heart.'"

Laura remarked, "Well, that child appears to have had a very wise, philosophical mother who taught her well."

"I know she talks about her mother with great reverence and respect. One thing that puzzles me, though, is the forgiveness and understanding she has for her grandparents—who refused to help her mother when she was in trouble."

"What about her grandparents on her father's side, can't they help?" Laura asked.

"I asked Liza that very same question and she said both her father's parents were dead."

"Poor little souls. When you think about it,

David, we are very lucky to be in the position we are in, and you were right that we have become less appreciative for what we have in life. Can you imagine what it would be like if our children had been born into the same circumstances as Liza and her little sister? I'll say one thing, David, young Liza certainly does make you grateful for what you have, and she certainly makes you think."

At that point Laura changed the subject. "Incidentally, David, the cook asked if she could see you about something private."

"What did she want to talk about?"

"I don't know, but it sounded quite important."

"Very well, let her know I'll see her in my study tomorrow morning at nine-thirty."

\* \* \*

At precisely nine-thirty the next morning, Mrs. Smith arrived at the Major's study. She appeared very excited, as though her news was of such great importance it might burst forth momentarily on its own.

Before the Major could even ask her what she wanted, she eagerly announced that she had talked to her daughter and her son-in-law, the Millers, about the predicament of Liza and her little sister.

"Sir, I talked to them for over two hours about the children and, they being childless, said they might consider taking them in as their own for a while, and see how they get on together."

"That is very Christian of them to even consider such a thing!" said the Major. "Have they any idea of the responsibility that such a decision would place upon them?"

"Yes, Sir, they do. I tell you, Sir, both of them have kind hearts, and they have wanted children for many, many years, but haven't been blessed with any, least-wise not yet.

"The way they see it, sir, adopting them children would be a godsend."

"Well, Mrs. Smith, this is a pleasant surprise! I will discuss the matter with Mrs. Rutherford, and then let you know if we can help in some way."

"Thank you, Sir, I just thought you and Madam would like to know."

"Mrs. Smith, I am overjoyed to hear such good news!"

\* \* \*

The Major was delighted by Laura's reaction when he recounted his conversation with Mrs. Smith. She was overjoyed! "I'm sure that if Mrs. Miller is anything like Cookie, the children could not have found a finer home!"

# Chapter 7

# The Millers

Three days later as arranged, Robert took the Millers to meet the children.

While Laura and the Major waited impatiently for Robert to return with his report about that meeting, they speculated on what Cookie's daughter and son-in-law would think about the children, and on what Liza and Jenny might think of the Millers. It was not until seven o'clock that evening that Robert was shown into the parlour.

"I beg your pardon, but I thought you would like to hear the good news about the children."

"Yes, of course, Robert," Laura said. "What can you tell us?"

"About the children, Madam, Mrs. Smith's daughter and her son-in-law fell in love with both the little blighters, they did."

"Tell us everything, right to the last detail," Laura requested.

Robert told them how they had come across Liza and Jenny playing with a group of children taking full advantage of the little bit of sunshine to be found in London at this time of year. "When they saw me they came running to meet us and greeted us with huge smiles! Little Jenny was fine but the bit of extra running made Liza cough somethin' terrible. She didn't sound too good to me, Madam, sounded like her lungs was bothering her again.

"Anyway, Sir, I introduced Mr. and Mrs. Miller to the children and explained to Liza the reason for their visit. Liza immediately invited us in. 'Would you like a cup of tea?' she asked us, just like she was a fine lady.

"Then Mrs. Miller says, 'We'd love a cup o' tea, wouldn't we luv?' And Mr. Miller answers her, he says, 'Of course we would, a good cup o' tea never hurt no one.'

"Liza said her mum used to say when someone who was sick asked for a cup of tea it was a sure sign that they were on the road to recovery.

"As you suggested, Sir, I took them some more chopped wood and some coal and got the fire going for them."

"Good for you, Robert. Now, tell us more about what happened at the meeting," Laura prompted.

"Well, Madam, Mr. and Mrs. Miller took me aside only one-half hour after we arrived and said they would love to look after both of the children—at least temporarily to see if they were compatible.

"They explained to Liza the benefits to be expected if she and her sister were brought up in a proper home.

"Liza agreed with them, saying it was a wonderful opportunity for both of them. However, Liza had quite a few questions of her own. She asked Cookie's daughter why she wanted to help her and Jenny.

"Such a direct question caught them off guard and it was quite a while before Mrs. Miller finally answered, 'Because we don't have children of our own and both my husband and I have a lot of love in our hearts that we would like to share with two children such as yourselves.'

"Then Mrs. Miller said, 'The way I see it, Liza, both you and Jenny would have a new father and mother to love you, and in turn we would be getting two beautiful children. Then we could be a proper family.'

"Then Mr. Miller joined in and said, 'Mrs. Miller and I would be honoured to share our home with you two girls. At least we could try it for a time and if you don't like living with us, Liza, you can always come back to where you live now.'

"Before Liza could answer, little Jenny piped up, 'Can we go out and play in the sun, now?' 'Of course,' Liza replied. 'Let's go play in the sun.'

"And that's just what we all did for about two hours. I tell you, Sir, Madam, it was a sight for sore eyes, it was. It touched something in my soul, to see them little blighters playing so happy!"

The Major had never seen Robert so animated and emotional, and shook his head in disbelief, wondering what had happened to this man. Robert was not his usual scornful self! He appeared to have lost his habitual skepticism and distrust, and his behaviour no longer reflected an attitude of disgust for humanity, an attitude that had in the past resulted in much self-inflicted pain. And believe it or not, he was now regularly seen going about his duties with a smile on his face. In the past this had been a very rare event, indeed.

It struck the Major that he'd never seen Laura so intensely interested in anything as she asked Robert to continue recounting his experiences of the day with the children.

"Well, Madam, Mr. and Mrs. Miller played with the children for a good two hours, then Mrs. Miller produced a cloth bundle of food and pastries from a basket she had brought with her and suggested they share a meal before they left. Those two little tykes really tucked into it, especially little Jenny."

"Do you think the children liked the Millers?" asked the Major.

"Oh yes, Sir. They took to 'em like a duck to

water and little Jenny took a fancy to both of the Millers right away."

"What about Liza, how did she handle such an experience?" Laura enquired. "It must have been difficult for her."

"Well, during supper Mrs. Miller explained to Liza that her husband had his own bakery shop and how they weren't too well off financially, but always made enough to make ends meet.

"Then Mr. Miller explained that the girls would each have their own bedroom and how his wife was not only full of love, but was the best cook in the whole of England."

"How did Liza react to that?" the Major enquired with a smile.

" Liza said she could see that both Mr. and Mrs. Miller had good hearts and agreed that an education for Jenny was most important. Then Liza mentioned to the Millers that her mum had been schooling her before she died and that she also felt that Jenny should learn to read and write. She told them that her mum always said, 'An education is good because it expands our minds and lets us see beyond what we already know.'

"Apparently she has quite a few of her mum's writings," Robert continued.

"What kind of writings?" the Major enquired.

"It appears, Sir, that Liza's mother was some kind of poet."

"Then what happened?" Laura asked.

"Well, Madam, Mrs. Miller held Liza's hand and

said, 'By the sound of it, Luv, your mum trained you well. Anyone can see at a glance that you're a good lass. Your mum must have been proud of you, bless her heart.'

"Then Mrs. Miller asked Liza if she and Jenny would like to come and see what could be their new home. Little Jenny pulled at Liza's dress, making it very clear that she definitely wanted to do that. Liza accepted the invitation and as far as I know, Sir, they are getting together this coming Sunday."

"That is jolly good news, Robert. If they need transportation, please see to it they get the spare carriage."

"Thank you, Sir, and good night, Madam."

# Chapter 8

# A New Home

The following Sunday, the thirteenth of December 1834, was a typical winter day in London—bitterly cold with just a touch of frost on the ground. Robert had readied the carriage and was taking Liza and her little sister to see what they hoped would be their new home. As the carriage turned the corner into the Millers' street, the girls could see Mr. and Mrs. Miller eagerly waiting outside the door to greet them. Mrs. Miller gave both girls big, welcoming hugs as they alighted from the carriage, then ushered them into a lovely, well-furnished living room with an enormous coal fire hissing and spitting in the fireplace.

As they took in their surroundings, Liza smiled sweetly, but Jenny grinned from ear to ear. Then the Millers asked Liza and the little one up to see their new bedrooms. Holding Mrs. Miller's hand, Jenny skipped up the well-polished wooden staircase with Liza right behind them. Robert, caught up in the whole proceeding, followed along. The first bedroom was Jenny's. It was a good-sized room with a bay window facing out to the fields and a few small buildings beyond. It was clean, and it had a four-poster bed with a colourful feather quilt and two plump, goosedown pillows. In the centre of the bed lay a brown, stuffed bear that Jenny noticed straight away. She asked Mrs. Miller if she could touch it.

"Of course, Luv, it's yours," Mrs. Miller replied. "Mr. Miller and me want you to have it, it's something we've had for a long time and we've been waiting for a little one just like you to give it to."

Later, when Robert reported the events of the day to the Rutherfords, he told them, "Little Jenny clutched at the bear like you wouldn't believe, and tears began to roll down her little cheeks. It was heartwarming to see the little mite so happy."

The Major was pleasantly taken aback by Laura's reaction as she sat crying softly and constantly wiping her eyes. Sitting and watching her, he couldn't believe what he was seeing. Laura was changing in front of his very eyes; the girls were affecting Laura just as they had affected both Robert and himself. It had been many years since he had seen Laura so happy and content with her life. The Major's wish that the old Laura would return some day was coming true. Then it struck him like a five-pound cannonball: he realized that he didn't want the old Laura and that he would rather have the one he was seeing now.

With tears streaming from her eyes, Laura broke the silence and asked Robert to continue his report, and to not miss the slightest detail.

Robert continued to relate the events of the day: Jenny's whispering into Liza's ear, "Is this really to be my room?" and Liza's assurance, "Yes, it's your bedroom if you really wish it." Then the little one crying, "I do, Liza, I do."

"How lovely," Laura commented as she wiped away tears with her handkerchief. "What about Liza's room. Tell us everything!"

"Liza's room was quite similar to Jenny's, only it was a bit larger."

Laura gasped, "Oh! How wonderful for the poor little souls."

Robert continued his story. "After the children had settled, Mrs. Miller asked them if they were hungry. Both said yes and Mrs. Miller gave them the feast of their lives."

Taking some papers from his pocket, Robert handed them to the Major explaining they were some of Liza's mother's writings. "Liza said I should give them to you, but made me promise that I would return them after you have read them."

"You mean there are a number of writings?" the Major asked.

"Yes, Sir, she said she had nearly a hundred of them, but because they remind her of her mother, and she takes such comfort in them, she couldn't bear to part with more than a few of them at one time."

"Thank you, Robert, I will make sure the papers are returned to Liza when we are finished. Good night, Robert, and thank you for your report."

"Good night, Sir, Madam."

All that evening Laura and the Major talked about the children's situation and both felt in their hearts that the Millers would provide a good home for the children.

The conversation also turned to the letters and writings that Liza's mother had left her. "It's obvious that Liza values them very highly and guards them very closely," the Major commented, "so much so she would only loan us a few.

"Shall I read one or two to you?" he asked Laura.

Laura straightened in her chair. "Please do, I'd love to hear them."

The Major opened the first letter. The paper was discoloured by time and, though Liza had preserved it as carefully as she could, it showed the signs of being frequently opened and refolded. He read:

My darling daughter Liza,

I leave you neither silver nor gold but something far richer than a king's ransom. I leave to you the knowledge that I had the good fortune to be blessed with.

Read carefully, my child, for this knowledge will guide you through life as it has me. These letters I leave you are all I have to give you apart from the few possessions we have in our home. But worry not, my dear child, within these writings there is knowledge beyond anything you could ever imagine; knowledge that will assist and guide you through life.

Since the beginnings of time such knowledge has been sought in many different ways in many different lands. This knowledge I leave to you cannot be bought for silver or gold. This knowledge I speak of lies within the very soul of all human beings. I know deep in my heart that you have had but a glimmer of this knowledge.

As you grow each day, this wisdom I speak of will grow with you and guide you to wonders beyond your imagination.

This I can tell you, my dear Liza. Those who have the ears to hear and eyes to see the true value of these writings have been blessed.

> Guard them with your life, my child, and never let anyone destroy them or alter them in any way.
>
> *Your loving Mum*

Wiping the tears from her eyes, Laura remarked, "How wonderful," then asked her husband to continue reading the other letters.

The Major's voice quavered as he began to read the second letter.

> My dearest daughter,
>
> I know deep in my heart that you are a born seer and in our short life together I have taught you, as well as I am able, to use your gift wisely. If you do these things I have taught you, if you continue to use your gift wisely as I have shown you, I know in my heart you will be well guided through this life and you will know the true meaning of peace and contentment.
>
> Sweet dreams my child and always remember: It is never too late to dream, and if your heart and thoughts are pure your dreams can come true.
>
> *Your loving Mum*

Trying to stifle her sobs, Laura asked her husband to continue with another letter.

*My dearest daughter Liza,*

*The moment you were born I knew you were blessed. In your short life I saw you grow ahead of your years and shine with the light of spiritual wisdom. Use your knowledge wisely my daughter and always remember:*

*Happiness does not depend on worldly possessions. Nay, my daughter, happiness lies deep in the recesses of your soul and emerges as a gift from heaven.*

*Never forget, one of the most fascinating and beautiful things in this life is realizing the powerful knowledge that lies within every person. Such knowledge turns the mere natural into the superior natural where all your happiness lies.*

*When you understand these things I say to you, my daughter, you will indeed be a queen.*

*Your loving Mum*

At this point the Major had to stop reading to gain control of the overwhelming emotions he was experiencing. Once he had regained his composure, he continued with the next letter.

My dear child,

One of the most beautiful things I can bestow upon you is the knowledge that love is the mystical key that opens the doors to the beauty and happiness you seek.

Love, my dear Liza, is a feeling that comes in many disguises. It may be caring for someone in need, loving your husband, loving your children, caring for and helping your neighbours and friends. Or it may be bringing a little joy to others who are less fortunate.

There is no end to the different ways to use this beautiful gift called love.

Love, Mum

The Major and Laura sat in silence for the longest time, not saying a single word, then Laura held her husband's hand as he continued reading the letters.

*My dearest daughter Liza,*

*In your short life you have seen many things and have learned much. Since you were but an infant I have seen you grow wiser and wiser each day of your life. You are indeed a joy to be with, you are the love of my life.*

*One thing that I would impress upon you, my dear daughter: No matter what conditions you may live in, always remember, with love and compassion in your heart you will be as rich as anyone on earth.*

*Again I tell you, look very closely, my daughter, at love and compassion for they are two magical feelings that will help guide you through life. Such feelings are more powerful than any king's army.*

*Always cast away bad memories that dwell in your heart from your past, for they will torment your soul. But if you can keep your mind clear of negative thoughts, such a state will fill your heart with the joys of living and guide you through life.*

*Love, Mum*

At this point, the Major's voice broke and he could no longer continue reading. Laura gently placed her arms around him and held him tight. David had never before felt this way and he certainly had never allowed himself to lose control in front of another. He worked to control his emotions and after a considerable time he heaved a great sigh, wiped his eyes and asked Laura if he should continue.

"Please do," she replied softly.

*My dear Liza,*

*Open your eyes and ears and immerse yourself in the spirit daily; let it guide you through the path of life and you will never stray.*

*When you do these things I ask of you, it is then you will understand how to do without doing and seek without seeking.*

*This, Liza, is a mystical state beyond the intelligence you now possess. I know you have had only a glimmer of its existence, yet it has bestowed upon you a very special gift. Never forget, always try to remember to be grateful for what you have, and then you will never miss that which you have not. This, dear daughter, is the pathway to contentment in this life.*

*I realize these words make no sense to you at this moment. But of this I am sure: some day you will understand and when you do, it will be a joyous day for both of us.*

*All my love, Mum*

Scanning through the last letter, the Major said to Laura, "This one seems to pertain particularly to us, and contains wisdom we really should heed."

Dear Liza,

I think you know that I believe you to be very special. I would suggest to you that your own inner beauty will increase and grow as you recognize the beauty in others. This quality may not always seem evident, but I believe you are wise enough to know that everyone has a spark of the divine spirit, which they need only allow to come forth. Try, my dear, if you can, to be kind and considerate to those individuals who have not been graced as you have. Know that although you may not always agree with their ways and their thoughts, they are probably struggling, in their own way, to achieve happiness. Your unexpected kindness may be the light they require to guide them to their own inner peace.

With much love, Mum

Laura commented, "How profound the woman's words are. Liza's mother must have been a very unusual person, though I don't maintain I understand her words completely. I would certainly like to read them again some time."

"That's precisely what I was thinking," replied the Major. "I have a feeling her words are trying to convey something which at the moment eludes me; at the same time they make me feel light-hearted and joyful."

Laura asked the Major if he had asked Liza any personal particulars regarding her mother.

"Yes, I did, and she answered, 'I don't rightly know, but some people claim my mother was gifted.' Of course, I made no reply to Liza's statement, fearing to harm a little girl's memories of her mother."

* * *

The following morning, the Major sent for Cookie. When she arrived in his study, all ruddy from the heat of the kitchen and puffing a little from the climb up the back stairs, he asked her to get in touch with her daughter and son-in-law. "Ask them if they would be kind enough to come to the house as I have a few details regarding the children I would like to discuss with them."

Two days later, Mr. and Mrs. Miller arrived at the mansion and they were immediately ushered into the study where the Major and Laura awaited them. The introductions were accompanied by much blushing and shuffling of feet by the Millers, who were a little uncomfortable. The Major made a few preliminary comments regarding the weather in an attempt to ease the situation. He then conveyed his and Laura's pleasure on learning that they wished to adopt Liza and Jenny. "It's admirable of you both to undertake such a thing."

"Well, Sir, Mrs. Miller and I see it as a gift from heaven."

"Can you afford such a gift from heaven?" asked the Major.

Mr. Miller explained, "I have my own bakery, Sir, and we always manage to make ends meet."

The Major continued, "Mr. Miller, what you are doing for the children is commendable and it shows me that both you and Mrs. Miller have genuinely warm and tender feelings for Liza and Jenny. It is because of your feelings toward them that Mrs. Rutherford and I would like to help you in some way with the children, and so we have decided we would like to give you the sum of fifteen guineas per annum for each of the children. We feel this will be sufficient money to help both the children get an education as well as assist you in their upbringing."

The Millers stared at Major Rutherford and Laura in surprise; Mr. Miller looked shocked while Mrs. Miller reacted with open-mouthed disbelief. Quickly regaining his composure, Mr. Miller replied, "We thank you for your generous offer

Major Rutherford, but I can assure you it is quite unnecessary. I am absolutely certain that Mrs. Miller and I can manage to support the children quite nicely from the bakery's income."

The Major acknowledged his belief that what Mr. Miller said was no doubt true, but went on to say, "I feel very strongly about this, Mr. Miller. It is kind of you and Mrs. Miller to assume responsibility for these children, but Mrs. Rutherford and I would be honoured if you would allow us to be of some little help, also. I'll have my lawyer make all the necessary arrangements within the next few days."

The Millers sat in silence as they considered the enormity of the Major's generosity. Finally Mrs. Miller spoke, tears overflowing her eyes and rolling down her cheeks, "It is very kind of you, Sir, to even consider such an offer. I can assure you we will do everything possible to make a good life for Liza and Jenny. Both Mr. Miller and I feel it a blessing that they have come into our lives."

"I know in my heart you will," answered the Major, "and that is why it is our privilege and honour to help you."

With that, the Major and Mr. Miller ended the discussion with a hearty handshake, and the two ladies shared a heartfelt hug.

# Chapter 9

# Liza Falls Ill

*O*ne week later, Robert was finally on his way to pick up the children and take them to their new home and new life. There was a slight dusting of snow on the ground that muffled the sound of the horse's hooves as they trotted over the uneven cobblestones. December's icy winds were relentless and the steam from Nell's nostrils made her nose appear to be on fire.

As he approached the derelict building that the children lived in, Robert became aware of an eerie silence, and the hair on the back of his neck stood on end. He dismounted and his feelings of uneasiness became stronger and stronger. Robert knocked on the door, but there was no answer. His feeling that something was wrong increased as he called out Liza's name and knocked a second time. Finally the door squeaked open and there stood little Jenny, shivering with cold.

"Liza is not feeling well, Sir; she couldn't get out of bed this morning."

Robert entered the room and went over to Liza's bed. One look and it was obvious that the child was extremely ill. Immediately Robert bundled Liza up in her blankets and directed little Jenny to collect their few possessions while he carried the older child to the carriage. Then, as quickly as possible, he made his way to the Millers' home where Mr. and Mrs. Miller waited impatiently.

Robert hurried into the house carrying Liza and informed the Millers of the state of her health. Without hesitation Mrs. Miller gathered Liza into her arms and took her to the upstairs bedroom while Mr. Miller donned his overcoat and hurried out to fetch the doctor. Robert, in his own gruff way, tried to comfort Jenny as she sat close to the fire to warm herself. "She's in good hands now, little one," he assured her. A quarter of an hour later, Mr. Miller puffed into sight with the doctor in tow and immediately showed him the way to Liza's room.

Nervously, the Millers and Robert waited for the doctor's report on Liza's condition, trying to distract Jenny by asking her to see if she could make out pictures in the coal fire. It wasn't clear how much Jenny understood of what was going on, but she was certainly aware that it was something out of the ordinary, as she kept asking, "Mrs. Miller, when can I go see Liza?"

After what seemed an eternity, the doctor appeared at the top of the stairs and asked Mrs. Miller if she would take Jenny to her room, but she simply took the child's hand while the doctor spoke.

Shaking his head from side to side, he said, "I'm afraid it is not looking well at all. The child's lungs are terribly congested and she is burning up with fever. I'm afraid it won't be too long, now. She's such a frail little thing, and I don't see how her body can take much more.

"I'm sorry, but I've done everything I can and there isn't much more we can do for her except pray."

When the doctor had finished speaking, Mrs. Miller led Jenny into Liza's bedroom and left the two girls alone together.

Liza held Jenny's hand. She smiled weakly and spoke quietly to Jenny. "My dear sister, you and I were blessed when God sent us an angel in the form of the Major who guided us to Mr. and Mrs. Miller who want to be your new mum and dad.

"I know they have lots of love in their hearts,

and will take good care of you. I want you to promise me that you will love them with all your heart and always be grateful to God for what he has bestowed upon us."

"Are they your mum and dad too, Liza?"

"No, my dear sister. Soon I will leave you and have a deep sleep for I must go on a long journey that will take me to my mum and dad who are in heaven."

Sobbing uncontrollably Jenny said, "I don't want you to leave. Can't we just go back to our own place? Everything would be all right like before."

"No, Jenny, you must stay here with your new mum and dad. And do you know, I heard your new mum say she was going to get you a puppy for Christmas? Isn't that wonderful Jenny? Imagine, you will have your very own puppy to play with."

With tears streaming down her cheeks, Jenny sobbed, "I don't want a puppy. I want to stay with you, Liza."

Holding Jenny tightly against her, Liza explained, "The love we have for each other will never really allow us to be separated. In spirit we shall always be together as long as you live."

While Jenny sat with Liza, pleading with her not to leave, the Millers saw the doctor off, and thanking Robert, told him he may as well go home too, as there was nothing more to be done.

Mrs. Miller then returned to Liza's room. Within minutes Liza had fallen into a deep sleep and appeared to be barely breathing. Mrs. Miller took Jenny downstairs and left Liza to rest. They sat quietly, not knowing what to say to each other, and then slowly, bit-by-bit, Mrs. Miller coaxed Jenny into a conversation about her life with Liza. They talked for a bit, and then Mrs. Miller put Jenny to bed.

As soon as Robert returned to the Rutherford house, Cookie bustled up to ask how the move had gone. She was horrified to hear of Liza's condition and immediately begged permission to have the evening off to help her daughter with Liza.

All that evening, Cookie sat with Liza and constantly sponged her forehead in an attempt to reduce the fever, but her temperature climbed higher and an eerie silence, broken only by the child's racking cough, settled over the house.

As the clock in the hallway struck eleven o'clock little Jenny came out of her room and crept down the stairs to sit on Mrs. Miller's knee. "I can't sleep, why can't I be with Liza?" she asked plaintively.

Giving her a big hug, Mrs. Miller explained that Liza wasn't feeling well and that she really shouldn't be disturbed.

Jenny jumped off her knee, insisting, "I have to talk with her, please!" then ran up the stairs into Liza's room where Cookie still sat, sponging Liza's forehead with a cool cloth. When Cookie saw Jenny she opened her arms to embrace the little girl. "Child, you should be in bed, do you know it is eleven o'clock and little ones like you should be in bed at this hour?"

"I want to be with Liza," Jenny insisted.

Wrapping a blanket around Jenny and giving her a big hug, Cookie suggested that she could go to sleep close to her sister. "Just mind you don't disturb her," she whispered as she watched the youngster settle in.

Mrs. Miller appeared shortly. "Do you think it will be alright for her to stay?" she whispered to her mother, indicating Jenny.

"Poor little soul doesn't know what's going on. Let's just leave her here; I'm sure she will soon be fast asleep."

After the two women left the room, Jenny held her sister's hand and kissed her cheek, repeating, "Liza wake up, please wake up. I feel afraid and lonely. I want to go home with you where we can be together again in our own place."

Liza's eyes opened and she squeezed Jenny's hand weakly, "My dear Jenny, this is your home now and I'm afraid we can't turn back the clock."

"But Liza, you promised me you would never leave me and if I stay here you must stay with me. You told me that our mum always said, 'If your heart was pure you could wish for anything and it will come true.' And my wish is, we can stay together for ever."

With very little strength left, Liza squeezed Jenny's hand and once again fell into a deep slumber. At this point Mr. Miller entered. He scooped Jenny up, blanket and all, and sat her on his knee to comfort her until she was asleep, then took the sleeping child to her own bed.

Mr. Miller joined his wife and Cookie at Liza's bedside knowing there was nothing they could do now but wait. Mrs. Miller leaned over Liza's bed and held her hand, which was absolutely limp. The profound effect of Liza's condition was obvious in the sad set of her face and tear-filled eyes. Even Mr. Miller's usually jolly countenance was overwhelmed with concern.

A half hour went by with no improvement in Liza's state. None of them wanted to bring up the subject of the inevitable outcome of Liza's sickness and not a word was said on that account. Mrs. Miller, continuously wiping tears from her eyes, finally murmured, "Bless her little heart, I'm glad she's asleep."

Cookie announced, "I think a good, hot cup of tea is in order! Sleep is the best thing for Liza now, and I think she can be safely left alone for a bit. Why don't the two of you go down to the living room and relax in front of the fire while I put the kettle on and fetch the tea?"

As they sat waiting for the tea, Mrs. Miller held her husband's hand, and said, "I feel so sad for that poor little blighter upstairs, and poor wee Jenny really has no idea what is happening."

Squeezing his wife's hand, Mr. Miller replied, "Jenny isn't simple minded, Luv. I think she has a very good idea what is happening. She's just not ready to give up."

As Cookie made the tea, she thought about the

manor house and how the staff would normally be getting into a happy Christmas spirit by now. However, as soon as Robert had reported Liza's illness to the Major, the repercussions had been felt throughout the entire house.

Cookie served the tea in absolute silence, then, before they drank, the Millers and Cookie held hands for a few moments of silent prayer. Mrs. Miller's soft sobbing was all that broke the quiet. Then, with a quavering voice, Cookie began, "Please Lord. As you are already aware, I don't ask you for very much, but this time I would be ever so grateful if you could spare this little child, Liza, who has brought so much love into the lives of so many people. With your help she has been guided into our lives and has a whole new life ahead of her. If you would grant me this one prayer I would never ask you for anything again. Never." Now both mother and daughter wept uncontrollably until they gradually calmed and again the house was quiet.

Cookie and the Millers fell into a quiet reverie, then were startled from their stupor by the grandfather clock as it chimed twelve o'clock midnight. On the twelfth chime they heard a slight noise on the staircase and, looking up, were amazed by the sight that met their eyes. Frail as a wraith, Liza stood near the top of the stairs in her long, white nightgown. Her voice was faint, but lucid, as she asked, "May I have a cup of tea, please?"

Mrs. Miller rushed toward her saying, "My

goodness, child, you should be in bed."

Mr. Miller was staggered by the sight of Liza standing there, asking for a cup of tea. But within seconds he regained his composure, went upstairs and snatched a blanket from the bed, then sped back to Liza, wrapped her up, and sat her on his knee in front of the fireplace, saying, "A good cuppa's on its way, m'luv." Overcome, he held Liza's light weight close; tears of joy welled in his eyes, then overflowed and streamed unashamedly down his face.

Mrs. Miller's face glowed with joy as she repeated over and over again, "Thank the Lord her fever has broken." Then she whispered, "I just knew, deep in my heart, that all would be well. I just knew it."

Cookie returned from the kitchen with Liza's tea and sat close to her as the child slowly sipped it. Not a word was said as the Millers and Cookie sat, stunned, trying to comprehend the blessing of Liza's sudden and unexpected recovery that had been bestowed upon them.

Liza drank half her tea then closed her eyes and fell into a deep peaceful sleep in Mr. Miller's arms.

"Here, Luv, give her to me and I'll take her up to bed," Mrs. Miller said. Just as she uttered these words a door upstairs opened and little Jenny appeared on the landing, asking in a hushed tone, "Why is everyone crying?"

Mrs. Miller put her arms out to Jenny and went to gather her up in her arms, explaining that they were tears of joy. "Do you know what, Jenny? Liza is going to get better; her sickness is almost gone."

Jenny's eyes opened wide and then she asked, "Is she really going to get better?" She quickly added, "I knew she would."

"Yes, Luv, your sister will soon get well, once we put some meat on her bones."

Jenny and the two women followed Mr. Miller up the stairs and into Liza's bedroom. Mrs. Miller tucked the blankets around Liza then kissed her forehead, saying, "Welcome home, beautiful one."

Then Mr. Miller kissed Liza's forehead and quietly said, "Sleep tight, Luv."

Cookie approached Liza's bedside and held her hand. "You are a very special young lady and, as sure as this is the year 1834, there was a miracle in this house tonight."

Cookie continued to hold Liza's hand as little Jenny held her sister's other hand. Bending over Liza she kissed her cheeks and told her, "Oh, Liza, our new mum says you're almost all better." By this time, little Jenny's emotions got the better of her and she began to sob again. But Liza had wakened as Jenny spoke. She lifted her arm, placed it around Jenny's neck, and kissed her little sister's cheek, saying, "Tomorrow we will talk." Then, exhausted, Liza again fell into a deep slumber.

* * *

Breakfast was served as usual at the mansion the next morning, but it was not the same. Neither the Major nor his wife felt like eating the fine meal before them—they were undergoing such feelings of intense helplessness. Their appetites had been destroyed by knowing that even with all their wealth, there was little they could do to help Liza.

With her eyes swollen from crying, Laura said, "It's so unfair, a little child like Liza shouldn't have to go through all this suffering."

Suddenly, there was a tremendous turmoil throughout the house. People could be heard rushing back and forth, footsteps sounded up and down the halls, hurried conversations could be overheard and sudden exclamations were quickly stifled to prevent disturbing the family.

"What in heaven's name is going on?" the Major asked his bewildered wife as they rose to their feet. The Major flung open the dining room door, and there stood Cookie, beaming with unreserved joy.

Wiping the tears that suddenly spilled from her eyes, her voice jubilant, she informed the Major and Mrs. Rutherford that Liza's fever had broken around midnight and that she was surely going to be well, adding, "She even asked for a cup of tea."

Laura threw her arms around the Major's neck and addressed Cookie through her sobs, saying, "I know it's a few days early, but you have just given me the best Christmas present I've ever had."

The Major thanked Cookie for bringing the good news and, following Laura's lead, wished her a very merry Christmas.

"Oh! By the way, Mrs. Smith, I take it that all that noise and commotion we heard just a few minutes ago was the servants' reaction to the news?"

"Yes, Sir, they were all so happy to hear that Liza would be well, they just couldn't control themselves. I'll remind them their behaviour should be a little more seemly."

"On the contrary, Mrs. Smith. I think their reaction entirely appropriate. And perhaps you could do me a little favour before you take your well-deserved rest. The estate agent will be giving out a little Christmas bonus for each of the staff, and I would appreciate your passing on that information for me."

"Thank you kindly, Sir. You are such a good, kind gentleman. Merry Christmas to you, Sir, Madam, and God bless."

*The end.*